Angela R. Edwards

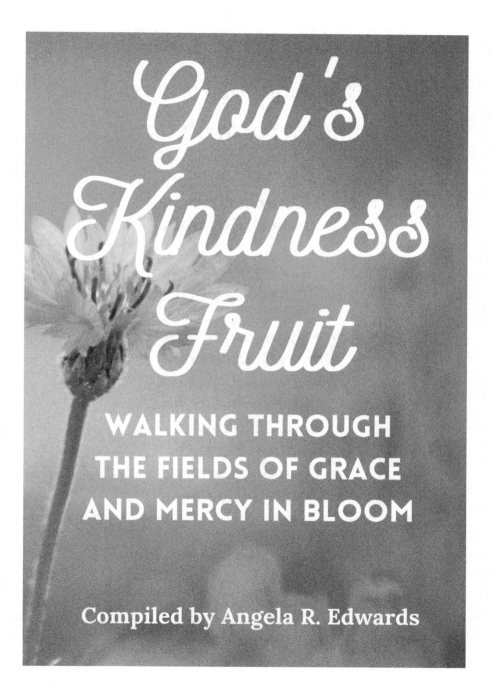

God's Kindness Fruit

WALKING THROUGH
THE FIELDS OF GRACE
AND MERCY IN BLOOM

Compiled by Angela R. Edwards

God's Kindness Fruit:

Walking Through the Fields of Grace and Mercy in Bloom

Compiled By:
Angela R. Edwards

Foreword By:
Marilyn E. Porter

Contributions By (in order of appearance):
Tosha R. Dearbone
Marlowe R. Scott
Reyna Harris-Goynes
Faith Makowa
Laurie Benoit
Precious Damas
Angela R. Edwards

Redemption's Story Publishing, LLC, Harlem, GA (USA)

Angela R. Edwards

God's Kindness Fruit: Walking Through the Fields of Grace and Mercy in Bloom

Print ISBN 13: 978-1-948853-70-5
Digital ISBN 13: 978-1-948853-76-5
Library of Congress Control Number: 2023946004

Scripture references are used with permission from Zondervan via Biblegateway.com.
Public Domain

For information and bulk ordering, contact:
Redemption's Story Publishing, LLC
Angela Edwards, CEO
P.O. Box 639
Harlem, GA 30814
RedemptionsStoryPublishing2020@gmail.com

Dedication

To those who value and practice kindness, please continue to sow those seeds in the world, as they are sure to grow into an orchard of kind acts, one at a time.

Kindness is never overrated.

Acknowledgments

First and foremost, all glory and honor are given to **God the Father**. Without Him and His guidance, this world would be lost...and unkind. Thank You, Lord, for Your precious Kindness Fruit.

To my supportive husband, **James Edwards**: I can never express enough how much you are appreciated. Thank you for filling in the gap as I worked to complete this project. Your meals were delicious! I love you!

To my children, **Anequilla Foots and Gerald Savage, III**: I am blessed to say I raised two very kind children. I love watching you both sow seeds of kindness into your own littles and how they interpret those teachings in their lives. Good job, you two! I love you both!

To my mother, **Marlowe R. Scott**: My goodness. I could—and need to—write a book on how much I appreciate you! Your years of wisdom shine through at every turn in my life. Your teachings have proven invaluable throughout my lifetime, and I thank you for being the epitome of kindness to our family and all those you encounter. I love you, Mom!

To my bestie, **Marilyn E. Porter**: Well, well, well... Here you are again! (Smiles!) After all that life has thrown at you, the kindness you display never ceases to amaze me. As we are nearing nearly half a century of friendship, I remain grateful for the authenticity you display and the shoulder you offer me to lean on at any given hour, no matter where you are in the world. I love you, Murl!

To the host of Contributing Authors of God's Kindness Fruit—**Tosha R. Dearbone, Marlowe R. Scott, Reyna Harris-Goynes, Faith Makowa, Laurie Benoit, and Precious Damas**: Thank you **ALL** for your unique stories! Without hesitation or excuses, each of you stepped up to the plate and swung hard, sharing words of encouragement for others to feed on in their lives. I pray your stories help at least one on their journey. Amen and *AMEN*!

Last but not least, to every person who has been kind to me without expectation of anything in return, thank you. I cannot begin to name all of you, but you know who you are, and you know the reasons why it was placed in your hearts to be kind. May you be blessed beyond measure today and always!

Foreword

Marilyn E. Porter

Dedication:
This is dedicated to the ones who have shown me kindness in every season of life.

Bio:
Marilyn E. Porter can be summed up in one word: Kind. She is the mother of three biological daughters—a number that increases when spiritual daughters are added. She is a preaching and teaching woman with a strong Apostolic mantle on her shoulders. She is a businesswoman, which encompasses being a Christian Life and Integrity Coach, Professional Speaker, Bestselling Author, Skilled Hybrid Publisher, and Business Consultant to both rising and seasoned entrepreneurs. Marilyn has the God-given ability to discern what others often need to see in both themselves and God's truth, operating in love and kindness all the days of her life.

Nice with pure actions behind it is the Fruit we call "Kindness." Perhaps an even better definition is "God is being nice to others *through* you." I assure you that you will not find either of those definitions in Webster's Dictionary, as they are purely my conversation takeaways with The Father. I had to learn that "nice" can be faked, while "kind" is a matter of the heart and will reveal itself through the authenticity of the act(s) of being kind.

At a very early age, I learned that "nice" and "kind" are not interchangeable. Nice is a form of societal necessity. If we are honest, we are most often nice when it is beneficial to our own needs or desires. Now, don't get me wrong: There is some merit to being nice to others, as it accounts for good manners.

As a child, I remember being told that I had to "be nice to others"—especially those who had the ability to be mean to me. Somehow, that just never made sense to me...not even as a child. Nice seemed to be a simple exchange of manipulations between humans.

I certainly understand why the Holy Bible does not list "niceness" as a Fruit of the Spirit. It is a manmade concept that allows us to be disingenuous to accomplish a mission.

I recall my family members referring to a man I once dated as being "a nice guy." I would always ask myself, *"Do they know how much trash he talks about them?"* and *"Do they know how* **NOT** *nice he is to me when nobody else is around?"*

So, it seems to me I have been defining "nice" and "kind" in my head and heart for many years.

Kindness is an act of humanity. It goes deeper than just human-to-human interaction. For example, we can be kind to animals, and they receive it as such.

When I think of kindness, my thoughts are immediately moved toward Jesus. I don't ever remember thinking one single time in my life, *"Jesus is so* **nice** *to me."* However, I have thought a million times how **loving** and **kind** The Savior is toward us.

I think of moments when I have been angry. I have never been able to be nice and angry, but I have been angry and remain kind. That is an act of love powered by grace. Kindness occurs naturally through the inner workings of the heart. Kindness is a luminous thread that weaves the fabric of human connection, embodying the essence of compassion and empathy. Kindness is the gentle force that propels us to reach out to others with warmth and understanding, irrespective of our differences.

A simple act of kindness has the power to uplift spirits, mend broken hearts, and forge bonds that transcend time and circumstance. Whether it's a smile shared with a stranger, a lending hand offered in times of need, or a comforting word spoken at the right time, kindness radiates a profound impact that ripples through our lives and the lives of those we touch. It reminds us of our shared humanity and our capacity to make the world a better place through acts of kindness, both grand and humble.

I appreciate this book and how it is solely based on the kindness of others. It allows me the freedom to rest in the fact that God is still here in the earth with us, and I can witness it through the kind acts of my fellow humans toward each other.

Introduction

In a world often filled with chaos, negativity, and divisiveness, kindness stands as a powerful force that can heal, unite, and bring light to the darkest corners. It is a simple virtue that can have a profound impact on both the giver and the receiver. On the pages of this book, we explore the transformative power of kindness and the ripple effects it creates in our lives and communities.

Acts of kindness come in various forms, from a warm smile to lending a helping hand, from a heartfelt compliment to a listening ear. Small acts of kindness have the power to uplift spirits, restore faith, and comfort those in need. Whether it's a stranger or a friend, kindness has the remarkable ability to make someone feel seen, valued, and supported.

Kindness also nurtures empathy—the ability to understand and share the feelings of others. When we practice kindness, we develop a greater awareness of the struggles and joys that exist beyond our own experiences. Being empathetic bridges divides and fosters a sense of connection and understanding. It encourages us to embrace our shared humanity and treat others with compassion, regardless of our differences.

When we extend kindness to others, they are more likely to "pay it forward," creating a chain reaction of goodwill. Simple acts of kindness, when multiplied, have the potential to transform communities, sparking a collective shift toward a more caring and compassionate society. Whether it's volunteering or perhaps initiating a grassroots initiative, kindness can be the catalyst for real change.

Yet another aspect of kindness is that it can strengthen relationships with family, friends, and colleagues. It fosters trust, deepens connections, and promotes a sense of belonging. By expressing genuine care and concern for others, we cultivate an environment of support and love. Through acts of kindness, we mend broken bonds and create lasting memories that enrich our lives.

Lastly, when we practice kindness, we experience a sense of fulfillment, joy, and purpose. It boosts our self-esteem, reduces stress, and enhances our overall mental and emotional well-being.

As you dive into the pages of this book, allow kindness to further cultivate qualities that this world needs now, more than ever—patience, gratitude, and forgiveness—for your personal growth and transformation is an ongoing process. If you find that a particular story isn't for you, you are encouraged to share it with others who may need a gentle reminder that kindness never grows old!

*"But the Fruit of the Spirit is love, joy, peace, longsuffering, **kindness**, goodness, faithfulness, gentleness, self-control. Against such, there is no law. If we live in the Spirit, let us also walk in the Spirit."*
Galatians 5:22-23,25 – NKJV (emphasis added)

Core Scripture

*"We then, as workers together with Him also plead with you not to receive the grace of God in vain. For He says: 'In an acceptable time I have heard you, and in the day of salvation, I have helped you.' Behold, now is the accepted time; behold, now is the day of salvation. We give no offense in anything, that our ministry may not be blamed. But in all things, we commend ourselves as ministers of God: in much patience, in tribulations, in needs, in distresses, in stripes, in imprisonments, in tumults, in labors, in sleeplessness, in fastings; by purity, by knowledge, by longsuffering, **by kindness**, by the Holy Spirit, by sincere love, by the Word of Truth, by the power of God, by the armor or righteousness on the right hand and on the left, by honor and dishonor, by evil report and good report; as deceivers, and yet true; as unknown, and yet well known; as dying, and behold we live; as chastened, and yet not killed; as sorrowful, yet always rejoicing; as poor, yet making many rich; as having nothing, and yet possessing all things."*

2 Corinthians 6:1-10 – NKJV (emphasis added)

"Just One" – A Poem

Angela R. Edwards © 2023

It's likely you've heard,

"Just one act of kindness can change the world."

I, for one, believe that to be true.

Were it not, what else would we do?

The polar opposite of kind is mean,

To the point it almost feels routine.

It doesn't cost a thing to be kind,

But there seems to be less of it on people's minds.

Let's come together on one accord,

Because believe it or not, we cannot afford

To let Satan continue to have his way

In our lives each and every day.

"Kill 'em with kindness!" is what I've been told.

That's advice that dates to the days of old.

If, by chance, you agree with me,

Let's practice "Just One" from now into eternity!

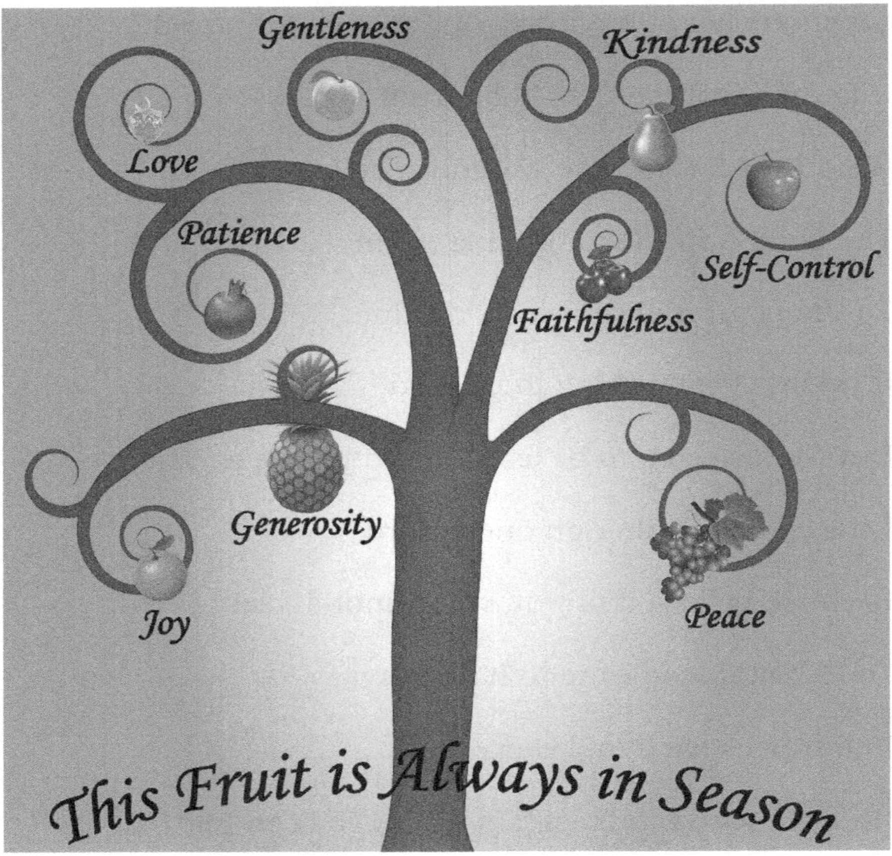
Gentleness
Kindness
Love
Patience
Self-Control
Faithfulness
Generosity
Joy
Peace
This Fruit is Always in Season

Table of Contents

Dedication vi

Acknowledgments.. vii

Foreword ix

    Marilyn E. Porter

Introduction xiii

Core Scripture xvi

"Just One" – A Poem xvii

Tosha R. Dearbone 1

    "When Kindness Tugs at Your Heart".............................3

Marlowe R. Scott..10

    "Kindness – Memories Linger".....................................12

"A Powerful Lesson from the Bees" – A heart-warming story

of love and care...17

Reyna Harris-Goynes..21

    "The Love and Kindness of a Child" 22

"Kindness' Poetic Glow" – A Poem 28

Faith Makowa 30

"Finding Hope and Embracing Kindness After the Loss of a Baby" 31

"Honoring the Memory" – A Poem.....................................38

"Kindness: The Children's Song" – A Poem 40

Laurie Benoit..44

    "Kindness: More Than Just a Word" 48

"Kindness Calms the Storm" – A Poem 58

Precious Damas 60

    "My Life, My Evidence, My Kindness Fruit" 62

"More Love into Life" – A Poem...66

Angela R. Edwards...68

   "The Seeds of Kindness" 71

Conclusion: Kindness' Ripple Effect 79

"Angels in the Air" – A Poem..81

"Kindness" – An Acronym 83

Journal the Power of Kindness...84

About the Compiler...95

Contact the Publisher...98

Tosha R. Dearbone

Dedication:

My story is dedicated to anyone who feels like life has been tugging at their heart and that no kind people are left. Know that there are still kind people in this world who truly care. Find those people and allow their kindness to embrace you.

Bio:

Tosha Dearbone was born in Urania, Louisiana, and raised in Houston, Texas. She holds many titles, including mother of four, grandmother of one, Community Advocate, Mental Health Aide, Founder of Positive Express, Certified Medical Assistant, Mentor, Author, and more. Tosha educates young ladies and women about HIV and AIDS, domestic and sexual violence, and self-esteem, and helps give voice to breaking generational curses. She found her passion for helping young ladies through her youth experiences and relationship with God. She can be reached on social media at Tosha R. Dearbone and via email at trdearbo@yahoo.com.

"Kindness Gonna Cost You" – A Poem

There is nothing like having a **"situationship"** tugging at your heart. You sit in silence and drift away, thinking of all the things you want to say. Sleepless nights and mindless thoughts even tend to get in the way. Without thinking, you begin to count yourself out and dim your light away. When others see you, they believe that all is okay. You try to smile, hoping kindness will shine a light on your day. You smile, wave, and even speak like nothing is wrong, but when you settle, your heart begins to tug away. Being kind can be hard when you are going through challenging situations but remember the light within that got you through all those other days "back then." Keep being a light in a dark world because you never know who will glean from your kindness to their own. Having a heart that tugs can be very devastating, but remembering The One who sits high can put kindness back in play.

If you had to make one wish today, what would kindness have to say? I woke up today. I get to start again. Don't take it for granted as you enter your day. Instead, lift your head and praise God that you can see another day!

Kindness is not something we can buy or pay our way into. Instead, God gifts us with this Fruit to be a light for others who seem to think that negative behaviors are the only way.

Be kind and hold tight to your heart so that it doesn't tug away!

"When Kindness Tugs at Your Heart"

Kindness... Being a kind, single woman in her 40s has been trial and error. Back in 2014, I took a break from being in relationships. However, it wasn't until one day, after being in an abusive relationship, that my oldest daughter said to me, *"Momma, maybe you need to be by yourself."* Those words didn't sound right to me at first because the thought of being alone sounded like abandonment, rejection, and even loneliness. My child wanted me to be without male companionship! I didn't hear her reason "why" until much later that day, but there was one thing I knew immediately: I needed to focus on myself, which meant doing some work! "Work" included digging up old feelings and past experiences and actually working towards healing.

"Work" also meant learning to love myself and getting to know **ME**—something I had never done before.

Growing up, my identity always felt disoriented. My mom was adopted, and my dad passed away when I was seven. That alone was already frustrating. My mom didn't talk much about where she came from or who she was, and I couldn't understand why. It took many years for small puzzle pieces to come together, but I understand why now. Early on, it felt as if she was living a secret life. However, I know she did her best by keeping my little brother and me around my dad's family so that we could at least have some semblance of a relationship with them. Still, it was hard living day to day without knowing who I was or where I had come from.

I remember trying to fit in with my brothers, only to be ignored and made to feel as though I didn't belong. That neglect led me to people-pleasing. I desired to be seen and heard by my brothers so badly that anytime they asked for anything, I gave it to them. Most often, that "thing" was my car. I would lend them my car without hesitation, hoping they would choose to hang out with me or treat me like a sister, only to realize later that it didn't make a difference. They continued to treat me as if I were invisible.

As time would have it, the years passed by, and being kind to everyone was all I knew. It not only made me feel good on the inside, but I also felt the Holy Spirit prompting me to be kind.

Mind you, as a child, I didn't know who the Holy Spirit was until the age of fifteen. I attended church with my friend and her mom and remember feeling

4

"different" on the inside. I couldn't put the feeling into words because I didn't want to seem weird, but there was no hiding the tears that fell or those times when my hands were raised in praise during service.

I thank God that I now know Him for myself and understand that His Spirit lives inside me. It seems I know no other way than to be kind to everyone. Yes, I have been in situations that may have called for a different response, but God always brought me back to His Fruits of the Spirit.

I recall the time back in 2020 when a new coworker came on the job. She had the most unusual character that would make anyone want to go **OFF** on her! She came in wanting everyone to acknowledge her, but it was done in the most unpleasant way.

*"If your brother sins, go and show him his fault in private; if he listens and pays attention to you, you have won back your brother. But if he does not listen, take along with you one or two others, so that **EVERY WORD MAY BE CONFIRMED BY THE TESTIMONY OF TWO OR THREE WITNESSES"*** (Matthew 18:15-20, AMP, emphasis added).

So, one day, the coworker and I had an encounter at the front end of our department, and she called me "the devil." **Babyyyy,** it took me back and caught me off guard. I quickly reminded myself that hurt people hurt people. As the day went on, her words still didn't sit right with me. The next day, I asked to talk with her one-on-one. I addressed the issue, and she explained why she called me "the devil" and behaved the way she did. She had no real reason other than I wasn't on her side—meaning she felt I should have agreed with her on everything because we were the same skin color. (She had me **ALL** wrong there!) Long story short, she appreciated me pulling her to the side to talk because (in her words) she "knew that I had a different type of spirit."

Let's return to me being single. At the time of this writing, I have been single for nine years but have started dating again the past couple of months. One day, a spiritual friend messaged me on social media, telling me that because I was single, I needed to be careful when ministering to men. Instantly, I had an "Ah-ha!" moment. Let me explain.

Throughout the past nine years, the men who tried to approach me gravitated toward me because they could see the new walk in my life and that I was vulnerable to the idea of being in a relationship. As I think about it, the same applies to my past relationships. I always treated my men with respect and kindness, which made it easy for them to misuse me. Some were intentional, while others recognized I was becoming aware of my true identity as both an individual and a child of God. That's where things sometimes got tricky. They would come in talking good, wanting me to share the Word with them, praying, etc. Then, they would play on that and pull me in when they saw how excited I became when talking about the Word. Again, some (not all) had an ulterior motive. While I was all in, I was mindlessly unaware of how they were just playing their cards until they could slide right into my bed after what appeared to be us in a committed relationship. In their defense, I don't believe they were "bad people." I just think they weren't ready to settle down.

Anyway, time and again, I was left feeling miserable. I allowed my kindness to interact with the enemy, triggering those past experiences I once held captive. I felt down and lost, as though I would never be in an authentic romantic relationship or get married.

So, I asked the friend, *"Why does this pattern insist on repeating itself?"*

She empathetically replied, *"You just have to be aware and careful moving forward."*

You know what? I agree! When using wisdom, I know I hear the Holy Spirit speaking to me about certain people and situations, but it's in my disobedience that I go left when God is telling me to go right. I must be more careful.

I share my story with you because I believe kindness is my portion and yours as well, but we—as humans—must use discernment and wisdom. Don't allow the enemy to catch you off guard. Being kind has taught me to see the good in others but not be blind or in denial of what they show you. The fact that others may mistake your kindness for weakness indicates that you may need to lean more on God's Word. That includes family and friends who mistreat you because they know forgiveness is dear to your heart. Don't be fooled. Be wise. The seeds you are planting in good soil will flourish!

Two quotes I live by are:

"Kindness is something anyone can give without losing anything themselves." ~ Author Unknown

"Kindness is not what you do, but who you are." ~ Author Unknown

Oh! And yes, I'm still waiting on my Boaz!

Marlowe R. Scott

Dedication:

To those who read these words, may you be blessed while appreciating the kindness received and give kindness, large and small, to others.

Bio:

Marlowe R. Scott has authored over a dozen inspirational books which earned Bestselling awards. Her books are now offered in a local Christian bookstore. She writes poetry, designs award-winning quilts, crafts dolls, and crochets. She is retired after many years of dedicated civilian service to the U.S. military, married, and a proud great-great-grandmother. Marlowe has written stories on each of the six Spiritual Warfare topics and is a contributing author to the Fruit of the Spirit series. Angela R. Edwards is her daughter and writer, editor, and publisher of this and countless other books. Marlowe's mantra is, *"To God be the glory for the great things He has done!"*

"Brighten Days" – A Poem

"Be **good**." "Be **nice**." Be **kind**."

Four-letter words everyone

Needs to keep in their mind.

Little words showing actions we are to do,

As we meet, greet, and join with family and friends,

And also strangers we may meet, too.

From childhood and the years that followed,

We heard "Be kind" at home, school, work, and worship.

We enjoy the kindness we receive with fond memories.

Our charge is to return this precious action to others,

As kindness is needed in our world in many ways.

"Kindness – Memories Linger"

The well-known hymn *Precious Memories* by J.B.F. Wright quickly came to mind when remembering the acts of kindness I have experienced. Although we may not always find kindness in everyday activities, it serves as a gentle, comforting, and warm feeling when received. Of course, things may happen throughout any given day to make thoughts and actions be the opposite. For example, some may say something out of line that goes against your morals, Christian views, and knowledge of God. What are you to do when those things happen?

Let's first look at a few other words for "kindness":

- Affection – gentle feeling of fondness.
- Courtesy – politeness in behavior toward others.
- Benevolence – well-meaning, forbearance, patience, self-control.
- Tolerance – gentleness; being kind, tender.
- Goodness – morally good or virtuous.
- Charity – voluntarily giving help to those in need.
- Hospitality – friendly and generous reception of guests, visitors, or strangers.

- Sweetness – pleasant, kind, and gentle toward people.
- Tenderness – gentleness and kindness.

Each word has been demonstrated toward me at least once, while their polar opposites have been used many times. For example, there were times when I was growing up when I was teased for being overweight, while others admired my long, wavy hair—and told me so. Occasionally, some people would add a "but" to their kind words, such as saying, "...but she needs to lose weight."

As a teenager, I had kind qualities that teachers, office personnel, and gym teachers recognized. I was courteous and maintained a helpful personality throughout my days while in school. As a result, I was chosen to be in the front row, dead center, to lead the voice choir in reciting Ecclesiastes 3:1-8! The third verse reflects the qualities, which are actions we may experience when we need kindness: *"A time to kill, and a time to heal; a time to break down, and a time to build up."*

I have had many people—not just family—who were nice to me throughout my life. As I have aged, the thoughts of those precious memories still bring feelings

13

of being loved, recognized, and cared for. As one of my former pastors used to say almost every week, *"It's just nice to be nice!"*

Now, as a senior citizen, memories flood my soul and mind of the kindnesses people have shared with me. One such instance was when I was loaned a car when mine broke down. That happened twice—by two different friends. I didn't even have to ask; they offered! I also recall times when I was shopping and didn't have enough money, and someone brought food to my home for my children and me without me asking. Then, some friends know my hobbies (crafting with flowers, crocheting, and sewing) and have given me gift certificates, fabrics, and more! I can safely say, **"My cup runneth over!"** I now have numerous boxes, storage bins, and shelves filled to my heart's content.

Each of the above instances highlights kindness, but I must let you know I am not just a receiver but a giver as well. As I am able, I give my time to support my church family with poetry, books, creative table decorations at my own expense, and teaching the preteens in bible studies. On one occasion, a young woman was devastated because of a personal problem. I held her hands, let her cry, and spoke to her about goodness while letting her know I was always available by phone or in person. She has since relocated and is happily married to a fine gentleman.

Reflecting on my time with the preteens, there were times when I had to be strict or give them a special "look" to get them in line, but to this very day, they still acknowledge me when we cross paths. When I attended church services, many would wave, come over to shake my hand, hug me, and more because I had somehow touched their lives or was extra nice and patient with them.

My three children have kindness in their character and interactions with others. Both boys are quiet but often volunteer to help in their communities and church. My daughter—who most may know is an author, book publisher, editor, and more in the publishing arena—is patient and kind by giving all the time needed for the authors under her care, many of whom end up on the Bestseller list on Amazon.

Resources for participation in acts of kindness are shared on TV, Facebook, and several religious and women's magazines, such as Woman's World, which has a section called "Circle of Kindness" that contains three acts of kindness in each issue. A recent act told of a couple, with the husband having painful arthritis in both knees and hips. After a doctor's visit, a woman noticed the couple struggling to make the trek back to their car, which was parked far away in a large parking lot. That stranger went and got her car, picked them up, and drove them over to their vehicle! Another story was about a woman who helped a young lady who needed help using a copier in a public library. While it may sound simple, I, too, was stumped when my local library changed its copy system. The third story was about a woman who needed a new iPhone. She was blessed when a former coworker gave her his old one—completely free—after he had upgraded his phone.

So, as you can see, **KINDNESS** is part of **EVERY** human being, although one's environment may sometimes cause it to be squashed or withheld. Those who are mentally, physically, or otherwise considered "not normal" have shown me more kindness than those from "normal" families, friends, and Christians.

This **Kindness Fruit of The Spirit** is easy to use. It's not difficult to share, and it's free! Why not think about someone who will appreciate your outreach of kindness? They will be blessed...*and you will, too!*

"A Powerful Lesson from the Bees" – A heart-warming story of love and care

Pen Drive © 2021

My dad has a hobby post-retirement. He has hives all over the place in his garden. And he collects honey. Not a lot, but enough to distribute to all his friends and relatives.

I make it a point to visit him whenever he collects honey.

A few days ago, I went to his house, and he showed me all the honey he had gotten from the hives. He took the lid off of a large pot, full of golden honey. All I could see on top of the honey was three little bees, struggling. They were covered in sticky honey and drowning.

I asked him if we could help them. He said he was sure they wouldn't survive and that they would be casualties of honey collection. I shuddered at the thought. Imagine one of us drowning in honey!

I asked him again if we could at least get them out and kill them quickly. After all, he was the one who had taught me to put a suffering animal (or bug) out of its misery. He finally conceded and scooped the bees out of the pot. He put them in an empty yogurt container and put the plastic container outside. They were still completely covered in honey and were slowly suffocating to death.

We put the container with the three little bees on a bench and left them to their fate.

Because my dad had disrupted the hive with the earlier honey collection, there were bees flying all over outside. They were worker bees—all of them females— who had worked tirelessly to build the hives and make honey. Now they had to go somewhere else to restart the entire process. Their life's work had been completely shattered by a thoughtless human being wanting their honey.

A little while later, my dad called me out to show me what was happening. The three little bees were surrounded by their sisters. They were cleaning the sticky, nearly-dead bees, helping them to get all the honey off their bodies and wings! Not even one had flown away in search of a better place to build new hives. Taking care of their siblings was far more important to them.

I watched in astonishment as two of the bees recovered sufficiently to fly. They did not fly away in relief, however. Instead, they turned around to help the last bee along with their sisters. After a few more minutes, the third bee had been cleaned and recovered enough to fly. That was the signal for the entire swarm to flap their wings and take off in harmony.

The container was now empty.

Those three little bees lived because they were surrounded by family and friends who would not give up on them...family and friends who refused to let them drown in their own stickiness...family and friends who had resolved to help until the last little bee could be set free.

Bee Sisters. Bee Peers. Bee Teammates. We could all learn a thing or two from these bees.

Why can't we be like these bees? Let us start at least from today.

Bee kind...always.

Story adopted from:
https://medium.com/age-of-awareness(c)/a-powerful-lesson-from-the-bees-4650bb5df9c5

Reyna Harris-Goynes

Dedication:

My story is dedicated to my children. Although I haven't been the best mother, I haven't been the worst. Just know that no matter what is said about me, I will always love each of you with everything in me. All of you are truly what makes my heart beat daily.

Bio:

Reyna Harris-Goynes is a wife, mother of five, and grandmother of two. She is also the proud owner of three businesses: V.R. Fashions & More, V.R. Fashions & More Online Boutique, and V.R. Mobile Notary. Her mantra is, *"Keep moving forward...daily!"*

"The Love and Kindness of a Child"

ditor's Introduction: In the bustling tapestry of human existence, some stories stand out like radiant beacons, illuminating the profound depths of love and kindness that reside within our hearts. The following story is one such luminary. It is a testament to a mother's unwavering devotion and the extraordinary kindness that blossomed in the hearts of her children. Although the world is often beset by chaos and discord, this tale serves as a poignant reminder that even amidst life's greatest challenges, love can shine brilliantly and inspire acts of kindness that echo through generations.

This story is written by a mother whose love for her children served as the catalyst for the extraordinary display of compassion and empathy that touches the lives of others. It's not just about her love; it's also about transforming her children into beacons of kindness. They exemplify the belief that when sown in fertile hearts, kindness can sprout into a force of immeasurable good.

We pray her story will touch your heart and inspire you to seek and nurture kindness within your own life.

****

When I found out I was pregnant with my youngest daughter, Rey'Lynn, I knew right away she would be someone special. Still, I wasn't at all prepared for what the good Lord gave me...and nobody else could prepare me for what to expect either. Rey'Lynn amazes me every day with the things she does and says.

I fondly recall how loveable she demonstrated herself to be toward others when she turned two. We could go anywhere, and she would speak to any and everyone. Often, she would receive happy responses from others. I enjoyed watching her interact with people she didn't even know. At the tender age of two, she had no idea how speaking to some people simply made their day!

Rey'Lynn is also a hugger—something else that puts smiles on countless people's faces. I smiled broadly as they expressed joy at her level of kindness, saying that she made their day. I've learned that when people encounter her, they adore her spirit. I've even received comments from people who say, *"That baby has been*

23

here before!" (I smile when I hear that because it's something I've heard since she was a mere six months old.)

Rey'Lynn is no ordinary child. She brightens up virtually anyone's day just by walking into the room. If you're in a bad mood, she's the one to brighten your day and make it a little better. I can bear witness to how her kindness and empathy make a grey sky turn blue. Sometimes, when I'm dealing with something challenging, she's so in tune with my mood change. She tells me, *"Everything is going to be okay, Mommy!"* Also, when my son was receiving chemotherapy, Rey'Lynn was by his side every step of the way. Although she's the little sister, she always ensured he was okay. I recall her brightening the doctors' and nurses' days as well! Without hesitation, she often puts others' happiness ahead of her own. I absolutely **LOVE** that about her!

My son, Keyonte, is quiet and laid back. There was a time, however, when he used to talk a lot, and, at times, I couldn't get him to stop talking! The change came when, in 2018, he was diagnosed with childhood cancer. That talkative child everyone knew had fallen silent. He distanced himself from the adults in his life but remained communicative with his peers. During our frequent visits to the hospital, he refused to talk to the doctors and nurses more than he had to.

After spending time in and out of the hospital for a few years, we built a bond with some of the doctors and nurses and have grown to care for them. There was a time when the Make-A-Wish Foundation sponsored a one-week vacation to Disney World for our family. While we enjoyed that much-needed getaway, seeing the many smiles on the children's faces made my days much brighter. I was hopeful that Keyonte would become more responsive immediately after that trip, but it was not to be.

I have not and will not put any pressure on him to step outside of his comfort zone. He's slowly coming around and talking to people other than just his peers, but we still have our work cut out for us. Even though he still doesn't speak much to the hospital staff, some people manage to get a smile or two out of him occasionally. I believe they know he cares when he flashes a dazzling smile at them during his visits. He's such a sweet boy and very kind. I love me some Keyonte!

My oldest children are amazingly kind as well. Even though I don't talk to them every day, I know they always got my back. They will also help others as best they can, even if they use their last to do so. We haven't always seen eye-to-eye, but how they interact with their younger siblings truly amazes me. When it comes to family, they are all in and make me so proud!

I did my best to raise my children. As we all know, parenting doesn't come with a manual. Much like other families, ours had many ups and downs. Thankfully, the good truly outweighs the bad. Loving and caring for children is a full-time job, but it's worth it. I'm reminded of the adage, *"Only the strong will survive!"*

The love between a parent and child is indescribable. So many have tried to come between my children and me, but they have failed because of the special bonds I have with them. My children are my life—always and truly forever, and more than they will ever know. They are my gifts from God!

****

Editor's Note: That story of a mother's love for her children, who exhibit remarkable levels of kindness, is an inspiring testament to the power of unconditional love and nurturing. Through their upbringing, Reyna has instilled in them the values of empathy, compassion, and selflessness. Bearing witness to their acts of genuine kindness towards others has filled her heart with pride and reinforced her belief in the innate goodness of humanity.

The bond between Reyna and her children is unbreakable, as they continue to support and uplift one another. As they grow into compassionate adults, their kindness begins to have a ripple effect, positively impacting the lives of those around them.

Allow this story to serve as a reminder that a mother's love can shape individuals who can make a profound difference in the world through their acts of kindness and empathy.

"Kindness' Poetic Glow" – A Poem

Angela R. Edwards © 2023

In a world so vast,
Where darkness may creep,
There shines a beacon,
A kindness so deep.
It's the gentle touch
That mends a broken heart,
The ray of hope
That ignites a fresh start.

Kindness
A currency of the soul
That knows no bounds
And makes us whole.
It spreads like wildfire,
Lighting up each face;
A warmth that no distance
Or time can erase.

With a single smile,
A bridge is built
Between strangers,
Uniting hearts without guilt.
A helping hand
Extended in times of need;
A testament to
Humanity's noblest deed.

Kindness speaks in whispers
But echoes loud.
In the hearts of the weary,
It lifts the shroud.
It's a gentle word
That mends the scars
And dissolves the walls
That divide us afar.

In the quietest moments,
It blooms and thrives,
Seeding compassion
In countless lives.
For even the smallest act,
The tiniest seed,
Can grow into a forest,
Fulfilling every need.

Let kindness be
Our guiding light,
In the darkest of days
And the blackest of night.
For in the realm of kindness,
We all belong.
A symphony of love,
Where compassion is a song.

So, let us embrace
This gift we possess
And let kindness flow,
Never settling for less.
For in each act of kindness,
We find our worth,
And transform this world,
Bringing joy and rebirth.

Faith Makowa

Dedication:

I dedicate my story to every woman who has lost a child prematurely through miscarriage or stillbirth. Although deep feelings of loss may always accompany you, remember always that you are a mother to your beautiful baby.

Bio:

Faith Makowa is a certified and licensed Institutional Counselor and Life Coach. She is the Founder of The Imprint Network, dedicated to connecting men and women in the process of rebuilding communities and connecting people. Evangelist Faith considers it a blessing to spread the Word of God through various means. She has co-authored several books as a way to share the goodness of God effectively. Faith has been married to her husband, Michael, for 22 years and is the mother of two sons. Between studying and sewing, she enjoys spending time with her family.

"Finding Hope and Embracing Kindness After the Loss of a Baby"

Editor's Introduction: Life can be a delicate balance of joy and sorrow, where moments of happiness are often accompanied by unexpected heartbreak. One such profound experience is the loss of a baby—a tragedy that leaves an indelible mark on the lives of those affected. In the following true story, Faith delves into the depths of grief and explores the transformative power of kindness in her journey toward healing and maintaining a healthy mental well-being.

Kindness towards oneself is the first step in navigating the complex labyrinth of grief. It involves allowing space for emotions to surface, honoring the pain, and embracing vulnerability. Faith finds solace, strength, and the ability to rebuild her life after loss through her courage to be compassionate towards herself. Her story serves as a poignant reminder that, despite the unbearable pain, it is possible to find light amidst the darkness and embrace a future filled with hope and healing.

****

My birth experience is a tale of trauma without warning. Since that day, I have been unable to experience full-fledged spring seasons or enjoy the sounds of birds chirping every morning. There was no goodbye...no moment of silence...not even a message. It was hard to understand the pain of knowing I carried a lifeless child in my womb for hours.

I kept thinking it was my fault, but God—in all His lovingkindness—reminded me never to give the enemy a seat at the buffet through the situation. Tribulations come to steal our precious joys and destroy our souls. But God!

Around 2:00 a.m., I was awakened by strong labor pains accompanied by heavy bleeding and cramping. Blood was spurting out, so I frantically jumped out of bed. At that moment, neither my mind nor heart were at ease. I felt like my world was turning upside down. Without wasting a second, my family rushed me to my local clinic for emergency assistance. By the time I arrived, the pain was unbearable.

I vividly remember the nurse yelling, *"It's an emergency!"* As I lay on a tiny hospital bed with my head elevated and nurses examining me, I heard one of them say, *"It's a serious placental eruption! The baby has no heartbeat!"*

That was followed by silence, which was quickly broken when another nurse announced, *"The baby is breached. Both mother and child are in danger of dying. Call an ambulance! We can save the mother."*

I was emaciated and weak when the ambulance arrived. They rushed me to the nearest hospital—about an hour's drive from the clinic. Along the way, my body discharged the placenta completely, leaving my unprotected baby inside my womb. The pain was **excruciating**! Although the EMTs had inserted an IV to transport water and nutrients through my weakened body, strength eluded me. I began to feel my soul leaving my body, with a great shadowy darkness overwhelming me.

The world I knew was no longer underfoot. The fear of death overtook my heart. I knew if I didn't get to the hospital on time, I was sure to rest in a dusty grave. I felt numb, and then a vision appeared before me...

I was carrying a bloody stomach as I climbed narrow, steep stairs in the dark. Then I heard screams in the distance, with someone calling my name. The place was foggy, humid, and windy. I stood in that place, chilled to the bone. It felt like winter. A very bright light illuminated my face as I slowly looked at the diamond moonlight, covered with a snow-white coat. The light penetrated and filled the darkness, forming a single line. I observed a group of people enter a beautiful glass corridor one by one. Just as I was about to join the line, I saw a sea of crystals and heard angels singing the old redemption song.

Indeed, God commanded His angels to guard me in all my ways. He knew my heart deserved happiness, hope, and healing. His deep voice called my name: *"Faith! My death has conquered death; you cannot now join eternity. Go back. I give you eyes of faith and ears to hear My steps."* His voice calmed my restlessness and confused thoughts. He clothed me with righteousness and gave me a new nature.

From a very high place, I saw my family and friends sobbing, praying, crying, and begging God for mercy. Then God's voice returned to me again, saying, *"Fear not; I will be with you, and I will bless you with many children."* Suddenly, a very big and bright star showed the way back to my family. Someone called my name, and I answered. When I opened my eyes, I saw many people gathered around my hospital bed.

"She' is awake! Call the doctor!" someone called out.

When I woke up fully, the doctor said, *"You just came out of the surgical ward and had a C-section."* I was thrilled to think that my child was alive! When I was about to ask for her, the doctor continued. *"We are sorry. We couldn't save your baby. We lost her."* I was so devastated, I couldn't even cry. (Those who have lost a child can understand. Even if you haven't, you can imagine.) Trauma is when sea billows roll through the painful stages of giving birth to a lifeless baby.

It seems like her innocent body was made for a specific sacrificial offering. Seeing her tiny nostrils covered in blood was a sign that our little girl was badly injured and traumatized before taking her last breath in the darkness of my womb. What remained were memories of my time carrying her and a suitcase filled with pink and white clothing. Her body was cremated. I could smell the flames of her body being burned in my thoughts, with the smoke filling the sky with a cloudy, dark smoke—a sign of mourning for those who loved her for the eight months I carried her.

Life was no longer a delicate rose bush filled with silky petals at that moment. Rather, it was a wavy leaf.

Death had become an integral part of life that had endured painful moments. I recall the flesh of my abdomen being zigzagged with stitches and scars from the surgery, yet my spirit-woman suffered immensely. That pain was invisible to the naked eye. However, God showed up and granted his gift of mercy. He covered my wounds and made them instruments of His glory.

Against all odds, I learned I was pregnant again five months after my stillbirth tragedy. My husband and I hadn't planned on trying again, but we learned we were pregnant three months in. Doctors suggested aborting the pregnancy because they believed I needed to wait at least two years because I was a high risk and could not carry a baby full-term due to an autoimmune condition that would have made it that much more difficult. But believe me, I have heard the mysterious mutterings of the forests about God and the winds singing praises as they stir the waters. I understood how the chorus of stars proclaimed His glory in the depths of infinite space.

After nine months, I gave birth to my sunshine baby without any complications. If I had agreed with everything the doctors said, I would not have witnessed the miracle of birth. Five and a half years later, we were blessed with another child.

GOD proved that doctors can never comprehend His mysteries. He is with us at every point in our lives, even when we are barely scraping by or discouraged after a season of loss. God always supplies our needs and reminds us of His love and kindness. If you have lost a child, may God place His healing hands upon you, making the sun rise and set again and blessing you with many children.

****

Editor's Note: Women who have walked the path—as shared in Faith's story—understand the significance of self-compassion and forgiveness, realizing that no one is to blame for life's tragedies. By embracing kindness toward oneself, a healthy space can be created for grieving, feeling, and healing. Through self-love and understanding, they can begin rebuilding their shattered lives.

You are encouraged to explore the critical role of kindness and forgiveness, whether or not you have lost a precious life. Be kind to yourself, embrace your emotions, and forgive yourself for not having all the answers. Through the journey, you will find healing, strength, and the courage to rebuild.

Always be kind...to yourself.

"Honoring the Memory" – A Poem

Angela R. Edwards © 2023

In the shadowed realm of sorrow's embrace,
Where tears of grief like silent rivers flow,
A parent's heart, once full of life and grace,
Now shrouded by a void, an endless woe.

A child, a precious light, forever gone,
Their laughter, dreams, and love a fleeting breath,
In the depths of darkness, we must don
To heal the wounds of loss, to conquer death.

Yet, in this desolate, unforgiving space,
Where pain unfurls its gnarled and heavy vines,
The ember of self-love must find its place,
A beacon through the darkest of confines.

For kindness to oneself, a gentle balm,
To soothe the scars, to mend the fractured soul,
In self-compassion, we find healing's calm,
In self-embrace, we find our hearts made whole.

The mirror reflects eyes, once bright and bold,
Now dimmed by sorrow's unrelenting weight,
But see the strength within, the stories told,
In every tear that falls, in every trait.

The echoes of their laughter still resound,
Within the chambers of your wounded heart,
A love so deep, a bond that knows no bound,
In every memory, they play their part.

Embrace the pain, the anguish, and despair,
For in those depths, the healing journey starts,
The heartbreak bears the seeds of love to bear,
And in its fertile soil, new life imparts.

You are not defined by sorrow's cruel hand,
Your strength lies in the love you still possess,
Within your heart, your child's spirit will stand,
A guiding light, a source of tenderness.

In kindness to yourself, you will find the way,
To mend the wounds and let your heart renew,
With every dawn, a chance for hope to sway,
As self-love's gentle grace unveils the view.

Though loss has cast its shadow on your days,
And tears may flow like rivers to the sea,
Embrace the love that's in your heart always,
And through self-kindness, find your way to be free.

For in the tapestry of life and death,
The threads of love endure, forever strong,
In self-love's light, you'll find your every breath,
A testament to healing, where you belong.

So, let the healing journey slowly start,
In self-love's arms, your heart will find its way,
To mend the wounds, to heal the shattered heart,
And honor your child's memory every day.

"Kindness: The Children's Song" – A Poem

Angela R. Edwards © 2023

In a world
where kindness should reign,
Children and adults,
a stark terrain,
Let's explore this truth
with poetic might,
How kinder the young,
in the softest light.

In innocence, children,
they do abide,
With hearts untarnished,
nowhere to hide,
Their laughter like bubbles,
light and free,
Spreading joy and love
for all to see.

Their eyes,
like windows to a gentle soul,
Reflecting a world
where love takes its toll,
Innocence whispers,
their spirits sing,
Of kindness and hope,
like the first days of spring.

They share their toys,
without a second thought,
In the playground,
no battles fiercely fought,
With tiny hands,
they extend their grace,
A warm, tender smile
on each little face.

But adults, alas,
as years accrue,
Can lose that kindness,
that childlike view,
Caught in the tangles
of life's demands,
Their hearts sometimes bound
by self-made bands.

Yet, in the depth
of every grown-up heart,
Lies the ember of kindness,
a vital part,
For life's lessons,
though they may be tough,
Can teach us to love, to share,
to be enough.

With time and patience,
adults can find,
That kindness is
the salve for the mind,
To heal old wounds
and break down walls,
To answer hatred's
bitter calls.

So, let us learn
from children's grace,
Their boundless love,
their tender embrace,
To be kinder adults,
each and all,
Breaking down barriers,
lifting a fall.

For kindness is not
a trait just for youth,
But a beacon of hope,
a beacon of truth,
A flame in our hearts
that should never fade,
A light in the darkness,
a debt to be paid.

In kindness, we bridge
the generational divide,
Uniting the young and old,
side by side,
So let us all strive,
both young and grown,
To make kindness our legacy,
forever known.

In the end,
it's clear to see,
Both children and adults
can set hearts free,
With kindness as
our guiding star,
We'll find love and peace,
no matter how far.

So, let us cherish
the children's song,
Their unwavering kindness,
so pure and strong,
And with open hearts,
let's all play our parts,
To keep kindness alive,
in all our hearts.

Laurie Benoit

Dedication:

My story is dedicated to all who need to be reminded that kindness often appears in the most dire and unlikely circumstances.

Bio:

Laurie Benoit is a wife, mother, and grandmother from Saskatchewan, Canada. She began her healing journey through her passion for writing and has since become an accomplished author with the release of her book, *The Transformative Power of "The Word,"* in 2019. She is also a co-author in the following: *God Says I am Battle-Scar Free: Testimonies of Abuse Survivors (Parts 4, 5, 6, and 7); God's Love, Joy, Peace, and Patience Fruit: Walking Through the Fields of Grace and Mercy in Bloom;* and *Poetic Voices: Seeking Solidarity During Racial Transitions.* You can connect with Laurie on Facebook at www.facebook.com/onceawakened.

"Reflections of Kindness" – A Poem
Laurie Benoit © 2023

As I ponder today
The days of my past,
Reflections of Kindness
In memories that last.

A simple lunch spared
For someone in need.
Who knew someone cared
When my heart did just bleed?

Scared and alone,
In a world unjust;
A heart torn between love
And knowing who to trust.

Kindness from a stranger,
An eerie feeling, indeed.
A heart sensing danger,
But my head says concede.

The love of a parent;
A new feeling to me.
The reason not so apparent,
Yet my heart wants to flee.

The warmth of a shower.
The softness of a bed.
In the late-night hour,
I often would dread.

Hunted and stalked;
An unwilling prey.
To a stranger, I talked
Until the light of day.

He said,
"I can help you,
Or you may end up dead."
Heavy in heart, I knew this was true.

So, I accepted a chance
On a stranger that night,
To take a firm stance
And put up a fight.

Fear overwhelmed me.
Shaking with dread,
His words were solid, a simple guarantee.
Now, if only my thoughts would get out of my head.

In the coming years,
Many words unspoken.
Plenty of anger and tears
From a girl who felt broken.

Many years down the road,
I continued to carry
The weight of my load,
A pain that was scary.

Many years later,
When rock bottom found me,
Into my life, she came for greater.
This time, I didn't flee.

Three little words
That found me silent one day.
Three little words
In my mind, to stay.

Life isn't fair.
You can learn that from me.
Do not despair,
For one day, you'll be free.

Reflections of Kindness
In days from the past.
Reflections of Kindness
In memories that last.

"Kindness: More Than Just a Word"

When I think about what kindness means and looks like in my life, it brings me a deep feeling of warmth and comfort to know there are people in this world who genuinely care. Although I have experienced many difficult and overwhelming moments of pain, I, too, have experienced the full depth of kindness in some of the most trying times of my life. I appreciate people who have stepped up to the plate when they simply didn't have to—people I consider to hold the highest integrity and care for humankind. Their actions speak louder than words and will echo through my thoughts for a lifetime. Because of those acts of kindness I received, I try my very best to ensure I pay it forward and treat others with the dignity and kindness they so richly deserve.

The very first act of kindness I recall experiencing was at a young age. To be precise, it was my very first day of school. I am certain that many people can relate to that unending fear of having *the worst* first day of school or work. For me, it was a reality. However, what the universe rewarded me with that day was something so rich it could never be replaced: the gift of **Friendship**.

It may be difficult for some to imagine how the small act of sharing lunch with someone could change their life, but for me, that is exactly what happened that very first day of school. For the first time in my life, I felt and was on the receiving end of kindness. The young girl who was so very willing to share her lunch with me that day, I repaid with a vow of eternal friendship. However, that would not be her only act of kindness toward me in the years that followed. In fact, I am not certain she truly understands the depth of how much her actions *saved me* for many more years to come.

See, I am a survivor of generational abuse. Escaping to school offered some reprieve from my daily terror. Because of what I endured on that first day of school, I quickly became a target for bullies. They knew nothing of my personal life but were definitely quick to judge. They first tormented me about my very embarrassing first day. Then they targeted my appearance (being a stalky, freckle-faced redhead with a boyish haircut). That was followed by being teased about the wardrobe hand-me-downs from my brother and the meager lunches I brought to school daily.

Oh! I must not forget the one thing that hurt the most: the endless years of teasing because of a last name I could not change until well into adulthood.

Those things might not seem like big things to fret over, but atop everything else I was coping with, they sometimes made my childhood almost unbearable.

That same young girl stood up for me and by me when nobody else did, and when she did, she did so with **kindness**. She spent every possible moment with me at school and continued sharing meals with me on days when I didn't have lunch to eat. Although she didn't know it, just being in her presence made me forget my usual horrors. Even though many years passed, and our lives took us in very different directions, my childhood friend and I managed to reconnect in adulthood and remain friends to this very day.

As the years progressed, the abuse I endured behind closed doors (that I remained silent about) grew progressively worse. I faced many more deep-rooted pains, including traumas, bullying, isolation, and leaving the family home and my one dear friend behind. The fact is I would not understand the word "kindness" again until my teen years. As a child and teen, I was always hopeful that perhaps one day, I would indeed find my forever family because the one I knew and had as a child, I honestly never felt as though I belonged. Perhaps it was the abuse, but even from my very first memories, I always felt out of place and unwanted.

The next memorable time kindness arrived in my life came by way of parental figures. Admittedly, I have always wondered why, in the short span of a few years, I had a few different couples who expressed interest in adopting me. Nonetheless, I welcomed and accepted their love and kindness. As I spent time with the couples who made efforts to adopt me, I began to feel hopeful that I might have a normal life in the future. First, one couple was denied, then another, and then came my very last hope: a couple whose truths touched me as deeply as my life touched them. They could not have their own children, and I was their last hope. At the time, I didn't know that they, too, were mine.

They had people of good stature with esteemed reputations supporting and guiding them through the entire process, so it truly was promising. They remained cautious about how they proceeded with our relationship and explained they would not introduce me to their family until everything was in the finalization phase. When they finally took that long-awaited step to introduce me, I felt confident I had finally found *my family*. I was welcomed with such deep love and acceptance that I felt like I was **home** for the first time ever.

But my life was no fairytale, and I did not get to live my happily ever after from that point onward. Instead, being denied the opportunity to adopt me ripped apart a loving couple—one that meant so very much to me. That same denial drove me into the depths of suicidal ideation, so much so that it nearly found me successful in taking my life. I fell into a deep depression for months to follow, and when I heard the reason behind the denial, I became enraged and loathed both the reason and the person behind it: my abusive father. The simple truth is I became enraged at the fact that he could say anything about it, as I had not been in his custody for years. I was, after all, a ward of the court.

As the years continued to pass, I carried that rage with me. I would not allow myself to express the pain, so I dealt with depression and eventually found myself living on the streets. Believe it or not, that was another place where kindness entered my life in a very profound way.

If you are unfamiliar with *"street life,"* let me explain: It is very much like any school or work environment. ***"The streets"*** contain cliques of people who generally run in the same circles, just on a larger scale. So, when you get in someone's way, you often get in the way of many. It can get to be very dangerous very quickly. Unlike at school or work, however, nobody can prevent a mob of people from coming after you should you get into an unpleasant situation.

In all my years on the streets, I found myself in a few situations where kindness was extended to me. Sometimes, it was offered as a warm place to sleep, a hot meal, a hot shower and clean clothes, home-baked goods, or even in the form of protection from *predators*— those who sought youngsters like me as a source of income for the illegal act of child trafficking. God forbid I refused to comply with "the norm" of others' expectations.

Well, with my unstable upbringing, that is precisely what happened to me.

Allow me to share a bit more of my backstory. I have always been the kind of person to never just **"accept"** a situation I viewed as unjust, abusive, or outright wrong. Looking back, I suppose that is partly why I have endured so much in this lifetime. I have never been a person who sits idly by and keeps my mouth shut. I am one who *"rocks the boat,"* even in my own life. When adding in the likes of someone else's mistreatment, I was definitely not one to keep my mouth shut. Because of that, I often paid for it in the long run.

The time came when I tried to befriend people to stand alongside me and fight back against a known child trafficker who was trying to loop me into his ring. I spoke with others outside his clique and was often met with people who did not want to fight simply because they struggled with surviving each day (much like me). Some didn't want to get involved because the trafficker was well-known and had dangerous contacts.

Nonetheless, I continued to reach out to others until suddenly, one of the most significant acts of kindness ever entered my life.

At the time, I was at a crossroads: I could take matters into my own hands and end the man's life and possibly spend the rest of my life in jail; I could have given him what he wanted (me) with the possibility of never being seen again; or (the option I hadn't seen coming) having an opportunity to break free from the streets with the help of one act of kindness.

I accepted the generous offer to break free, which began yet another lifelong friendship. To this day, I herald that act of kindness as the most significant in my life.

Fast forward from 1986 to a little over 30 years later—five years ago at the time of this writing—when I found myself on the receiving end of kindness yet again.

As an adult, I still felt lost, hurt, betrayed, and uncertain about where to turn in the small community where I had thrived for many years. See, I had spent an entire lifetime building a career in retail, and although it is not a highly sought-after career because of the poor wages and lack of benefits at the time, it is physically demanding, and sometimes, you must contend with unhappy customers. It was a career in which I thrived because I loved the variety of tasks.

After four years of working in a local store, it changed ownership. I decided to continue working there until everyone I had initially worked with left. Things seemed to escalate quickly after that, but in reality, it was two-and-a-half more years later. I remained working there until I was eventually let go. In the months leading up to my dismissal, I had been bullied. While my boss was away on holiday, my bullies concocted their final plan to get rid of me. What followed was a list consisting of 22 complaints "apparently" filed against me, including telling people I refused to be of service to shoving people into shelves. I was in a state of shock as I read the list of lies! It was a real blow to my overall well-being. I couldn't believe my 20-year career went down the toilet in one fell swoop.

Then came the most recent acts of kindness that graced my life. Two separate individuals who didn't have to stand up and say anything **DID**, simply because it was the right thing to do. It helped to remind me once again that true friends are the people who say good things about you behind your back. It made me recognize that the respect I held for those individuals before had changed to a deeper level and that sometimes, even when people don't outright announce they are your friends, when times are tough, they simply stand up and prove it.

So, may we always be reminded to spare a bit of kindness to each person we meet, for it might just save a life!

"Kindness Calms the Storm" – A Poem

Angela R. Edwards © 2023

In a world where harsh words often sting,
Where anger and bitterness take their swing,
There lies a lesson, both simple and profound,
To be kind to those whose hearts are bound.

When unkind words like arrows fly,
And venomous barbs make hearts sigh,
In the face of anger, let kindness bloom,
For kindness can lift the darkest gloom.

When someone's hurting, though they may not show,
Their pain and struggles, the battles they go,
Extend a hand, offer a gentle word,
In kindness, let your voice be heard.

For in the tempest of anger and despair,
A seed of kindness can mend and repair,
The wounds that fester, the scars that bind,
A chance for healing, for hearts to unwind.

It's not always easy, this path we choose,
To be kind to those who abuse and accuse,
But in our kindness, we hold the key,
To break the chains and set hearts free.

For those who hurt, often hurt inside,
Their pain hidden well, their tears denied,
In the midst of their storm, extend your grace,
A beacon of kindness in their troubled space.

Instead of fueling the fires of strife,
Let kindness be the rhythm of your life,
A counterpoint to anger's bitter song,
A chance for reconciliation, to right the wrong.

You see, kindness is a powerful force,
It can alter the course of a bitter discourse,
It can soften hearts, mend what's torn,
And in the end, a new day is born.

So when faced with words that wound and scar,
Remember, kindness can go so far,
To heal the wounds and calm the storm,
To bring about a heart's transformation.

In being kind to those who hurt and hate,
You break the cycle, you dissipate,
The darkness that threatens to consume,
Replacing it with love, in kindness' bloom.

For in the end, it's not weakness to be kind,
But a strength of character, a noble mind,
To rise above the hurtful words and strife,
And in kindness, offer the gift of life.

So, when unkindness comes your way,
Let kindness be your choice, come what may,
And in that choice, you'll find the way,
To change the world, one heart a day.

In the face of anger and hurtful words,
Let kindness be the song that's heard,
And in that melody, let healing start,
A testament to the goodness in your heart.

Precious Damas

Dedication:

To all the little lost girls who need someone to hug and love them, my story is dedicated to you. You are loved, brave, worthy, and beautiful! You are a survivor!

Bio:

Precious Damas is a child of God, wife, mother of three, and grandmother of six. She was born and raised in Boston, Massachusetts, where she had an amazing childhood. She has traveled the world, including visits to Germany, Texas, Georgia, and Florida. Precious is a newly published author of the International Bestselling *Mask Off: Two Faces* book series. Her mantra is, *"At the end of the day, I've loved and lost, yet I still push on."* You can connect with Precious by visiting www.facebook.com/MaskOffSeries.

"I'll Hold Your Hand" – A Poem
Precious Damas © 2023

It's okay, Ma. I'll hold your hand while Jesus holds the other.

You are my mother; there is no other.

You birthed me, fed me, and clothed me.

You taught me everything I needed to know from head to toe.

You showed me right from wrong as I came along.

You even taught me a song:

"Jesus Loves Me, This I Know."

When you punished me, it was for my good.

I knew you would, so there I stood—taking it like I should.

Your LOVE and KINDNESS got me through the hood,

And for that, I am grateful, thankful, and proud to say,

"Mommy, I love you and miss you."

Without a second thought, I want you to know

I keep you close to my ♥.

In loving memory of my mother,

Barbara Ann Barton.

R.I.P. 3/27/22

"My Life, My Evidence, My Kindness Fruit"

Age 15. 1:45 a.m.

"*I'm so hungry,*" I heard Simone say as I awakened out of my sleep. I should have gone home. At least the crackheads would have let me sleep because they were too busy trying to get that next hit. I could have been in my room with the door locked, safely tucked away. *"Yo, let's go down to Shaken and get some food,"* she suggested.

I was wide awake by then, but not because I was hungry. I was upset because it was almost 2:00 a.m., and my friends were out of their minds if they thought I was about to get dressed and walk down the hill to get food at two o'clock in the morning! The streets didn't love me **that** much. *"Naw. I'm good. I'm not hungry,"* I replied—knowing darn well I was after smoking weed and waking up from a long nap. They didn't need to know that, though. I wasn't going, and that was that!

Simone was the type of person who thought she was the boss of everyone. She wasn't the boss of me, though. Maybe she was over the other two, but not me. I had made up my mind that I was not going with them. After all, I was tired! I rolled over, and the trio left the room, only for Simone to return and say, *"Well, if you're not coming with us, then you have to leave my house."*

"You don't have to tell me twice!" I got up, threw on my jeans and t-shirt, grabbed my white Reeboks, and bounced. Part of me wanted to wake her mother on my way out, but I decided I wanted nothing more to do with Simone ever again, so I just walked out the door and never looked back.

As I made my way down the hill, I prayed to God—even though I didn't really know how to pray. I asked Him to see me home safely. Around 3:00 a.m., I arrived at Badge Station. I was happy to see it lit up and directly across from the police station. I figured I would be safe and that people would start coming into the station to go to work, so I wouldn't be alone. Sadly, I was **WRONG**. No one showed up. I was cold, scared, and angry.

While waiting, I noticed a car entering the station, which was odd because the area was only for buses. The vehicle circled me two times. Before it could do so a third time, I made a beeline for the police station. I knew I could trust them because they were there to protect and serve. Once I made it, I looked back and no longer saw the car. I entered the police station and explained that my "friend" kicked me out of her house because I wouldn't go with her to get food at two o'clock in the morning. The officer just looked at me and shook his head.

"Honey, she's not your friend," he said. *"Wait here. I'll give you a ride home."* I was so relieved and grateful for the officer's kindness.

While riding in the front seat of the police car, my mind raced. I thought to myself, *"Why aren't I in the back seat? Oh, my God! He's going to try to touch, kill, or rape me and get rid of my body!"* I prayed again, silently asking God to see me home safely. God did just that. I was never so happy to be home! I kindly thanked the officer for the ride home and ran into what I call **"The House of Horror."**

It was 4:00 a.m. when I entered my mother's house. My mom and her friends were wide awake. Everyone stopped what they were doing to look at me as I walked straight to my room. I shut and locked my bedroom door. ***"I'm still hungry,"*** I whispered in frustration while climbing onto the top bunk.

The next morning, I slowly rolled over and found one of my mom's friends asleep on the bottom bunk. I laid on my back and thought, *"What kind of ish is this?*

How could she? How could my mother allow someone to invade my space?"

Eventually, I got up and began to prepare for the day ahead, only to receive a phone call from one of my friends telling me that another of my friend's brothers had been killed the night before. My mind returned to the kind police officer who brought me home. If he hadn't given me a ride, he could have saved that young man's life or even stopped it from happening.

At that moment, I was so angry with Simone. I felt I could never forgive her for what she did. I wanted to blame her for everything that happened that night, yet I somehow knew God would not have wanted me to do that. Instead, God would want me to be kind and forgive her for what she did. He would want me to clothe myself with compassion, patience, and kindness.

It took me some time, but I did forgive Simone, and we have remained friends to this day. I honestly think that whole ordeal has taught me humility, which is why I am the person I am today.

In the end, you discover who is fake, who is true, and who would risk it all for you. By God's Kindness Fruit, you will recognize them. Every good tree bears good fruit, but a bad tree bears bad fruit.

"More Love into Life" – A Poem

Angela R. Edwards © 2023

In a world where conflict often takes its toll,
There's a lesson in kindness, a story to extol,
Of reaching out to those who don't share our view,
For kindness can mend what's been torn in two.

When faces turn cold, when eyes meet with disdain,
When others dismiss you, cause you hurt and pain,
In the face of such trials, let your heart find its way,
To be kind to those who, for now, choose to stray.

For kindness is a beacon, a guiding light,
That can bridge the divide, even in the darkest night,
It's a language universal, understood by all,
A path to mend the fences, to break down the wall.

When they throw stones, and their words are unkind,
When they judge without knowing your heart and your mind,
Stand strong in your kindness, don't stoop to their low,
Let your kindness be the river, let it steadily flow.

For those who dislike you may have wounds of their own,
Hidden battles, struggles, seeds of resentment sown,
In their hearts, they may carry burdens unknown,
So be kind to them, and let love be shown.

It's not about winning, or proving a point,
It's about being kind in every joint,
Of your life with theirs, in each interaction,
Choosing kindness over anger's infraction.

When they speak ill of you, with words that sting,
Remember, kindness has a soothing wing,
To heal the wounds, to ease the pain,
And in that act of love, much can be gained.

For kindness can disarm the sharpest blade,
Turn foes into friends, make hate start to fade,
It can plant a seed of change within their soul,
And eventually make the broken heart whole.

So, when faced with those who don't like your way,
Let kindness be your guide, come what may,
In every word and deed, let it shine,
A beacon of hope in a world less than kind.

It takes strength to be kind when others are not,
To forgive, to love, to hold the hurt at bay,
But in the end, it's the greatest prize you've got,
To touch a heart, to brighten someone's day.

In the end, it's not about them or you,
But the kindness you choose in all that you do,
To be a reflection of love's endless sea,
For in kindness, we find our truest victory.

So, when faced with those who don't like your name,
Let kindness be your legacy, your claim to fame,
For in kindness, we rise above the strife,
And bring a little more love into life.

Angela R. Edwards

Dedication:

I dedicate my story to the loving memory of my always kind father, **James Boyce**. His love and kindness are remembered by many.

Bio:

Angela R. Edwards is a woman of God, wife, mother, and doting grandmother. Born and raised as a "Jersey Girl," she currently resides in the balmy state of Georgia with her husband, James, and precious furbaby. She is the Owner of Pearly Gates Publishing and Redemption's Story Publishing, and the Founder of the Battle-Scar Free Movement—a nonprofit that addresses domestic violence and abuse head-on while providing resources for victims and survivors to thrive after abuse. Angela loves life, loves to smile, loves her family, and practices kindness at every turn. Her mantra is, *"Love life, and it will love you back!"*

"Kindness' Light Upon Your Face" – A Poem
Angela R. Edwards © 2023

In a world where shadows often hide the light,
Where hearts grow cold, and day turns into night,
There blooms a truth, a message pure and clear,
To be kind to all, both far and near.

In the garden of our souls, seeds we sow,
Of kindness and love, let these virtues flow,
For every creature, great and small,
Deserves our care, our love on each to fall.

In the footsteps of the Savior, we tread,
Whose love for all, in every word he said,
He healed the sick and gave the blind their sight,
His love, a beacon in the darkest night.

With gentle hands, we touch the wounded hearts,
With open arms, we offer a fresh start,
To animals and people, both in need,
In kindness, love, and grace, we plant the seed.

The sparrow's song, a melody so sweet,
In fields and forests, all God's creatures meet,
From lions' roar to dolphins' joyful play,
In every heart, love finds its way.

For in the eyes of every living thing,
A spark of the divine, a song to sing,
A reminder that we are not alone,
In this grand tapestry of life, we've grown.

Let's be kind to people, near and far,
To lift them up, to heal each hidden scar,
For in each face, a reflection we will find,
The Creator's love, so tender, so kind.

And to the creatures of the earth and sky,
Let's promise to protect, not make them cry,
For in their eyes, a trust that we must keep,
To guard their homes, even in the oceans deep.

Let compassion be our guiding star,
No matter who we are, no matter how far,
For in kindness, we find our truest grace,
A glimpse of heaven's love, a warm embrace.

So let us be the hands that mend and heal,
The hearts that understand what others feel,
And in our actions, let love brightly shine,
As we walk this path, both yours and mine.

In being kind to people and to creatures too,
We find our purpose, our calling to pursue,
For in these acts, our faith is truly shown,
The love of Christ in us, forever known.

In every moment, in every place,
Let kindness be the light upon our face,
And in this journey, let us humbly pray,
To love and care for all, come what may.

"The Seeds of Kindness"

As I sat with the task of writing my kindness story, the first question that came to mind was, *"What is in a name?"* My parents named me Angela. Many interpretations include "Angel" and "Messenger of God" in the description. I must say that I appreciate the name more now than I did in my early years. Why? Because in the 1970s, it seemed every other little girl shared my name! While that may be a bit of a stretch, I can easily recall six other peers named Angela when I was in grade school. How could I feel my name was "special" when so many others likely felt the same?

A visit to MyNameStats.com provided some pretty interesting information regarding my name: *"Based on the analysis of 100 years' [sic] worth of data from the Social Security Administration's (SSA) Baby Names database, the estimated population of people named ANGELA is 616,521."* See? Pretty common, right? LOL!

Enough about that. I want to focus on the "Messenger of God" message for my kindness story.

Outside of Satan and his minions who were cast out of Heaven, when you think of God's messengers, what image comes to mind? Do you envision angelic beings? Pastors? Evangelists? Missionaries? What about ordinary people—like you and me? As God's messengers, we are tasked with being kind, for we know not how our kindness will be received at any given moment in others' lives. That one act of kindness just may save someone's life!

Notably, random acts of kindness have been in the spotlight for nearly three decades. I used to wonder, *"What took so long to bring such positivity to the forefront? What happened 30 years ago that made it a **necessity** to bring attention to being kind?"* I'm kind and often go out of my way to help others, and I've experienced countless occasions where kindness was granted to me. Hmm... **What happened?**

In my story, I will share one instance when I was kind and another when kindness was shown to me. I hope and pray that the words penned on the pages that follow will inspire self-reflection and nudge you to be more aware of your kindness level daily.

Kindness Given

My parents raised my brothers and me to be givers, not takers. At every turn, both demonstrated how giving can be life-changing for both giver and receiver...when it's not taken for granted. In particular,

72

my mother tends to smile from ear to ear when she has given from the depths of her heart. In turn, the receiver recognizes the "gift" and often gives her something in return. Although that is **NEVER** the intention, that giving—that act of *kindness*—has a ripple effect that makes the giver feel good (and perhaps obligated in some form or fashion). My father was a giver in many ways, but one of the most memorable is how he often gave hitchhikers rides (this was **LONG** before it became hazardous to do). While it may appear to some that picking up hitchhikers does not demonstrate "giving," I implore you to think about it like this: On the hottest or coldest day of the year, a car ride could be a Godsend! With those positive influences in my life, how could I not grow up to **#BeKind**?

Let me ask a question that might cause you to think back to an earlier time: Were you ever kind to someone who didn't deserve it? That's the focus of my giving kindness story.

When I was a teen, we relocated to a brand-new home in a relatively established neighborhood. It didn't take long to make friends with the neighborhood children, especially those who lived directly behind us. Many days, I would walk through the woodsy patch that separated us to spend time with the three sisters who lived there.

In my junior year of high school, the oldest sister decided she wanted to fight me after school based solely on a **rumor** that I said something about her boyfriend. I'm one to tackle situations head-on, so I approached her in school to find out what in the world was going on. She snapped and yelled, ***"I'll see you when we get off the bus!"***

Well...

That afternoon, when we got off the bus at our stop, nearly the entire bus emptied, awaiting the "big fight." Imagine the onlookers' disappointment when they observed a lot of screaming back and forth but no fight. As you might imagine, visiting my other friends (her sisters) was no longer an option because "she" was there. Tension remained high between us because she chose to believe the rumor, even after she learned the truth: I **never** said anything derogatory about her boyfriend. Through it all, I managed to remain close to her middle sister all these years later.

Fast forward a few years. We are now adults and no longer living with our respective parents. The same girl who wanted to fight me and refused to mend our broken friendship despite my best efforts needed somewhere for her children to stay for a few days while she got on her feet. Her parents and sisters had moved out of town, and her other so-called friends couldn't (or wouldn't) help her. Imagine my surprise when I received a call from her, asking for **MY** help!

As much as I wanted to tell her no, I couldn't. We were both adults, with children and a past long forgotten. To add to it, I stopped and thought: What if it were me in that situation? I would want someone to help me!

Long story short, I took her children in for just over a week. Did we ever speak about the past? No. Did she ever apologize for the drama? No. Did I forgive her anyway? **Yes.** Remember: Forgiveness is for you, not necessarily the other person. It paid to be kind to her because, sure enough, there came a brief moment in time in my life when I needed similar support, and my son's maternal grandmother stepped up for my children and me without hesitation. I dare to imagine my fate had I not chosen to practice *kindness* with my former neighbor in her time of need...

Kindness Received

This next story is one I pray I never forget. I may forget my name one day, but I never want to forget the kindness of another neighbor when I was a single parent.

There was a time when my children and I were living on the brink of poverty. The light bill was overdue, the water bill wasn't paid, and the refrigerator and pantry were empty. I recall being grateful that my children were getting free breakfasts and lunches at school because I had to work diligently and creatively to give them some semblance of dinner when that time came. If it was hot dogs and beans, Ramen noodles, or a bowl of cereal, I ensured they ate something before going to bed every night.

Well...

There was one weekend when I was all tapped out. I had nothing to feed my children. **NOT. A. THING.** Meanwhile, my next-door neighbor was living it up. He had a barbecue that Saturday, with the cars wrapped around the block from the number of people in attendance. The yummy aromas found their way through the cracks and crevices of my home, making our tummies rumble. I prayed and then assured my children that God would make a way out of no way—which He did!

As the festivities next door began to wind down, a knock came at the door. It was my neighbor. I recall his exact words: *"I have a lot of food left over from the barbecue. I would appreciate it if you and your kids would help me eat it."* He followed that up with a hearty laugh simply because the request seemed silly when he put it that way. I laughed with him, of course, but in my spirit, I was praising God for His provision in my time of desperate need.

I waited until his guests left and then went over to help him clean up and pack up the food. When we were done, he flashed the biggest smile I have ever seen and said, *"All of this is yours. I don't want it. I don't need it. Make sure you and your children enjoy my good cooking!"* I gratefully accepted his offer, called my children to help us gather the food to take to our house, and then sorted and froze meats, vegetables, and sides galore!

Are you ready for this? The amount of food he gave us lasted for **TWO WEEKS**, which was just enough time for my next paycheck to come!

I am brought to tears as I sit and reflect on that day. God miraculously provided for us. The kindness my neighbor showered upon us was nothing short of a miracle. He didn't have to do it, but he did. He could have sent everyone home with plates, leaving nothing behind. He could have thrown away the food (wasteful, but it was an option). He could have offered what he gave me to someone else, but he didn't. **GOD CHOSE ME**, and I am forever grateful for His favor.

Perhaps you now see why I pray never to forget that story. Time and again throughout my life, the seeds of kindness sown and received have sprouted and grown into an orchard, bearing fruits that nourished my soul. I am constantly reminded that in a world often clouded by darkness, the smallest gestures of goodwill can ignite a spark that illuminates the lives of many.

The seeds of kindness are contagious, spreading like wildflowers in a barren field. I pray that you will cultivate a garden of kindness and transform your life, community, and, ultimately, the world...*one kind act at a time.*

Conclusion: Kindness' Ripple Effect

Small acts of kindness can brighten someone's day. Those seemingly insignificant gestures can create a domino effect, inspiring others to "pay it forward." Holding the door open for a stranger or buying a meal for someone in need can have a ripple effect, as the recipient may be inspired to do the same for others if they are able. That chain of kindness can nurture a sense of connection and empathy within communities.

Numerous studies have shown that acts of kindness release endorphins, reducing stress and improving one's health. Engaging in kind acts can boost self-esteem and enhance mental health, promoting a sense of purpose and fulfillment. Additionally, acts of kindness have been linked to improved cardiovascular health and lowered blood pressure, placing emphasis on the benefits of cultivating a kind heart.

When kindness becomes the norm, individuals feel supported and valued, creating an environment conducive to growth and positive interactions. Fortunately, kindness knows no boundaries or borders.

It has the potential to transcend cultural, religious, and societal differences, uniting humanity under a shared sense of compassion. In times of crisis, acts of kindness shine brightest, as people come together to support and uplift those in need. By practicing kindness on both an individual and collective level, we can create a ripple effect that spreads far beyond our immediate surroundings, ultimately shaping a more empathetic and harmonious world.

Kindness is not a mere nicety; it is a powerful force that can reshape our world. By embracing kindness in our daily lives, we can inspire others, nurture personal well-being, and foster a global community built on compassion and understanding. Let us strive to make kindness a guiding principle, knowing that even the smallest act can make a significant difference.

Together, we can create a brighter, kinder world, one act of kindness at a time.

Angela R. Edwards

"Angels in the Air" – A Poem

Angela R. Edwards © 2023

In the bustling streets of life we roam,
Amidst the crowds, far from our home,
A lesson whispers, soft and wise,
To be kind to strangers, a sweet surprise.

For in their faces, unknown and new,
Lies a mystery, a chance to renew,
The kindness sown in this earthly flight,
Could lift a soul to wondrous height.

They walk among us, these strangers near,
In the guise of people, they may appear,
But in their hearts, a secret they bear,
Perhaps, just perhaps, they're angels in the air.

In random encounters, on pathways crossed,
We find these strangers, never truly lost,
For in their presence, a message hides,
To be kind to all, where love abides.

In the eyes of a stranger, a world unfolds,
Stories untold, and dreams untold,
A simple smile, a gesture of grace,
Could brighten their journey, in this vast space.

Their needs may vary, their hopes unique,
Yet in kindness, our purpose we seek,
To offer solace, to lend a hand,
In this shared moment, to understand.

For kindness knows no bounds or face,
It fills the gaps in the human race,
And in these strangers, we may find,
A reflection of love, in humankind.

So, let us be kind to each passing soul,
For in their presence, a part of a whole,
In strangers, we may glimpse the divine,
A chance to be angels, in our time.

In the tapestry of life, they play a part,
These strangers who touch our fleeting heart,
And as we walk this journey's span,
May kindness guide us, hand in hand.

For in being kind to strangers, we see,
The potential for love and unity,
And in these moments, small but bright,
We become angels, in love's pure light.

"For His merciful **kindness** *is great toward us, and the truth of the LORD endures forever. Praise the LORD!"*
Psalm 117:2 – NKJV (emphasis added)

"Kindness" – An Acronym

Marlowe R. Scott © 2023

K – Keeping a positive outlook

I – In every day of our lives and

N – Never forgetting good feelings

D – Developed through receiving nice words or actions

N – Necessary or not a quick "Thank you" is said and

E – Emanating from your face is a nice smile.

S – So, as you enjoy acts of kindness, remember to

S – Share kindness, both large and small.

The **KINDNESS** Fruit of the Holy Spirit
is to be shared by all!

Journal the Power of Kindness

In the section that follows, you are encouraged to journal the acts of kindness both given and received daily for **30 days**. Prayerfully, you will reflect on those kind moments for years to come and be empowered to "pay it forward" at every given opportunity.

_____

_____

_____

_____

_____

_____

_____

_____

_____

_____

_____

Angela R. Edwards

_____

_____

_____

_____

_____

_____

_____

_____

_____

_____

_____

_____

_____

_____

_____

_____

_____

Angela R. Edwards

About the Compiler

Angela R. Edwards is the CEO and Chief Editorial Director of Pearly Gates Publishing, LLC (PGP) and Redemption's Story Publishing, LLC (RSP)—Award-Winning International Hybrid Christian Publishing Houses located in the Central Savannah River Area of Georgia. In May 2018, PGP was honored as the 2018 Winner of Distinction for Publishing in South Houston, Texas, by the Better Business Bureau (BBB). From 2019 to the present day, she has been a recipient of BBB's Gold Star Certificate for both entities for her exemplary service to the community.

Angela lives by *"My Words Have **POWER!**"* Since its inception in January 2015, PGP has been blessed with an ever-growing and diverse group of over 100 authors who have penned topics related to faith, love, abuse, bullying, Christian fiction, Bible study tools, marriage, and so much more. Their youngest author is two years old; their eldest is 82 at the time of this publication. To their credit and God's glory, PGP and RSP have collectively over 150 bestselling titles to date, including a series penned by Mr. Jimmy Merchant, formerly of the 1950s Doo-Wop group, "Frankie Lymon & The Teenagers," with their most recognizable music hit, *Why Do Fools Fall in Love.*

An affordable publishing option (in comparison to some of the large, traditional publishing houses), PGP and RSP work one-on-one with authors, ensuring that financial hardship is not a discouraging part of the publishing process. For those desiring to share their God-inspired messages, to include both new and seasoned authors, both publishing houses provide unique services and support that many have said "left them feeling as if they were the only author" placed under each company's care.

The Holy Bible states that *"God loves a cheerful giver"* (2 Corinthians 9:7). To that end, PGP and RSP are frequently hosting fantastic giveaways. Throughout the past few years, new author contests have awarded authors over $18,000.00 in services total.

In addition to the aforementioned, Angela is a domestic abuse survivor. Since first telling her abuse survivor story publicly, she has become a 'Trumpet for Change.' She is the Founder of the Battle-Scar Free™

Movement—a nonprofit that provides resources to abuse victims and survivors as they transition to a life free from abuse. As part of her God-given mission, she provided abuse victims and survivors a FREE opportunity to anonymously share their testimonies in a seven-book series titled God Says I am Battle-Scar Free. Although the series is complete, Angela's mission to help individuals heal with the power of their words continues. Assisting others with the healing process is paramount to her, which propelled her into volunteering for two years at the Star of Hope Mission in Houston, Texas, as their first-ever Domestic Violence Liaison.

Angela holds an A.A. Degree in Business Administration from the University of Phoenix and is pursuing her B.S. Degree in Psychology with a concentration in Christian Counseling from LeTourneau University. She is a woman of God, wife, mother, grandmother of 22, and trusted friend. Originally a New Jersey native, she has since made Georgia her home and embraced the southern culture in all its fullness.

Angela loves life and affirms daily: ***"NOT TODAY, SATAN, AND TOMORROW ISN'T LOOKING TOO GOOD, EITHER!"***

Contact the Publisher

Pearly Gates Publishing and Redemption's Story Publishing are always looking for new talent and desire to "birth the writer" in **YOU**! Will you be next on their list of Bestselling Authors?

Contact us today!

Visit PGP on the Web at PearlyGatesPublishing.com

Visit RSP on the Web at Redemptions-Story.com

Connect with PGP on Facebook at
PearlyGatesPublishing

Connect with RSP on Facebook at
RedemptionsStoryPublishing

Email Angela Edwards, CEO, at
pearlygatespublishing@gmail.com

Call 832-994-8797 to schedule a
FREE 15-minute publishing consultation.

****

The Battle-Scar Free™ Movement
can be found on the Web at
Bsfmovement.org
and on Facebook at
Bsfmovement

Made in United States
Orlando, FL
31 October 2023

38407906R00068